YASHIMOTO'S LAST DIVE

ANTONY TREW

YASHIMOTO'S LAST DIVE

ST. MARTIN'S PRESS
NEW YORK

Library of Congress Cataloging-in-Publication

Trew, Antony, 1906–
    Yashimoto's last dive.

    I. Title.
PR9369.3.T7Y37   1987   87-16306
ISBN 0-312-01116-4

First published in Great Britain by William Collins Sons & Co., Ltd.

First U.S. Edition

10 9 8 7 6 5 4 3 2 1